Keiki's First
WORD BOOK

Library of Congress Catalog Card
Number: 2004102696

ISBN-10: 0-9729905-5-0
ISBN-13: 978-0-9729905-5-4

Edited by David Del Rocco

First Printing, May 2004
Second Printing, February 2005
Third Printing, June 2006
Fourth Printing, March 2010

BeachHouse Publishing, LLC
PO Box 5464
Kāne`ohe, Hawai`i 96744
info@beachhousepublishing.com
www.beachhousepublishing.com

Printed in Korea

Keiki's First WORD BOOK

illustrated by Lance Bowen

BEACHHOUSE
Publishing, LLC

My ʻOhana (Family)

mom
makuahine

bird
manu

sister
kaikuahine
kaikua`ana
kaikaina

brother
kaikunāne
kaikua`ana
kaikaina

dog
`īlio

baby
pēpē

auntie
`anakē

cousin
hoahānau

grandma & grandpa
kūpuna

cat
pōpoki

dad
makua kāne

uncle
`anakala

In My Hale (House)

table
pākaukau

window
pukaaniani

quilt
kapa kuiki

mirror
aniani

lamp
kukui

desk
pākaukau hana

chair
noho

plant
mea kanu

picture
ki`i

bed
moe

rug
moena weleweka

sofa
kokī

door
puka

What Should I Wear Today?

hat
pāpale

sunglasses
makaaniani lā

shorts
lole wāwae
pōkole

dress
lole

t-shirt
pālule

slippers
kalipa

swimsuit
lole `au`au

socks
kākini

raincoat
kuka ua

shoes
kāma`a

pajamas
lole moe pō

aloha shirt
palaka aloha

Outside in the Garden

rake
hao kope

butterfly
pulelehua

hibiscus
aloalo

bird
manu

cockroach
`elelū

umbrella
māmalu

ant
naonao

swing
lele

frog
poloka

plumeria
melia

gecko
mo`o

palm tree
kumu niu

Let's go, go, go!

motorcycle

mokokaikala

truck

kalaka

skates

kāma`a holo
pahe`e

bus

ka`a `ōhua

taxi

ka`a ho`olimalima

baby stroller

ka`apēpē

skateboard

papa huila

bicycle

paikikala

train

ka`aahi

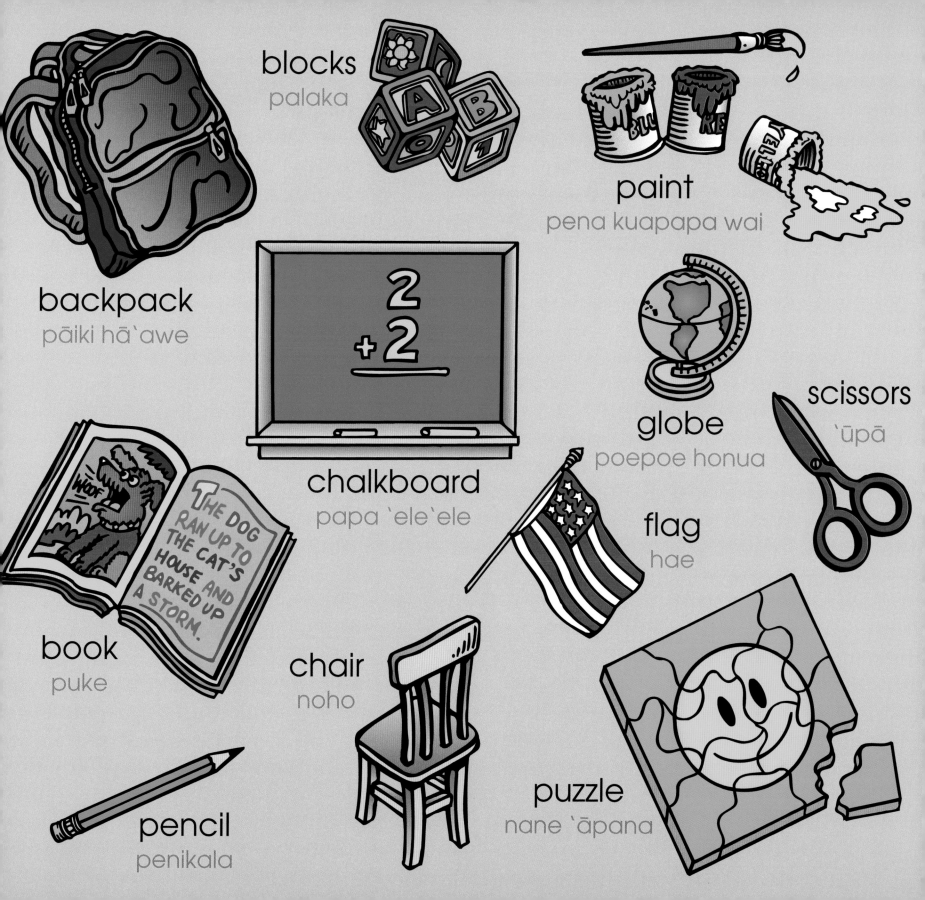

blocks
palaka

paint
pena kuapapa wai

backpack
pāiki hā`awe

2
+2

globe
poepoe honua

scissors
`ūpā

chalkboard
papa `ele`ele

THE DOG RAN UP TO THE CAT'S HOUSE AND BARKED UP A STORM.

flag
hae

book
puke

chair
noho

puzzle
nane `āpana

pencil
penikala

Only in Hawai'i

waterfall
wailele

`ukulele
`ukulele

volcano
lua pele

pier
uwapo

Diamond Head
Lē`ahi

rainbow
ānuenue

cliff
pali

beach
kahakai

canoe
wa`a

hula
hula

lei
lei

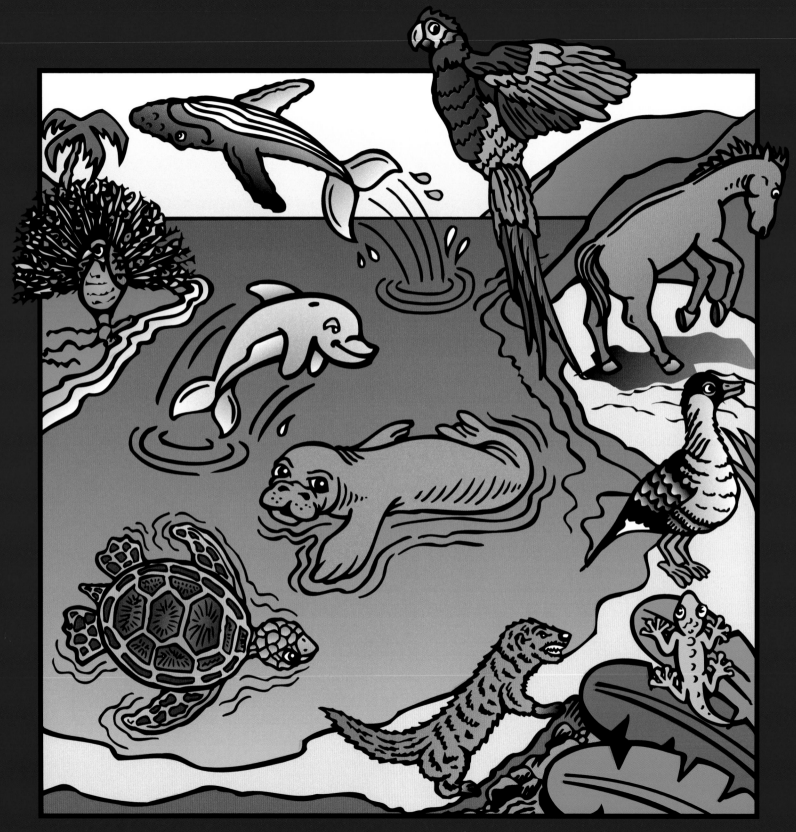

Hawai'i's Special Animals

whale
koholā

gecko
moʻo

horse
lio

dolphin
naiʻa

mongoose
manakuke

turtle
honu

parrot
manu
aloha

peacock
pīkake

goose
nēnē

seal
ʻīlio holo i ka uaua

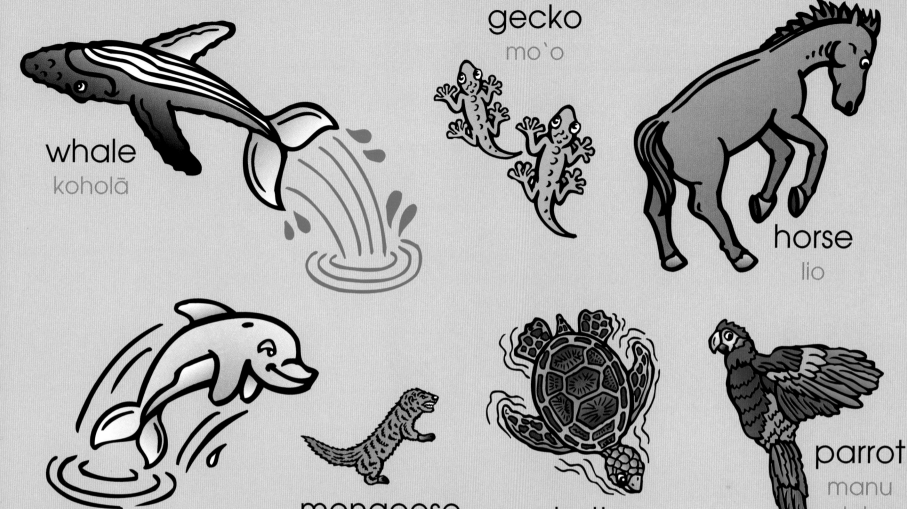

drum
pahu

gourd
ipu

singer
pu`ukani

chanter
mea oli

hula
dancer
mea hula

`ukulele
`ukulele

conch shell
pū

guitar
kīkā

`ulī`ulī
`ulī`ulī

towel
kāwele

shovel
kopalā

slippers
kalipa

shell
pūpū

ball
kinipōpō

facemask
makaaniani lu`u

crab
pāpa`i

bucket
pākeke

surfboard
papa he`e nalu

mat
moena

sandcastle
kākela one

Things In the Ocean

boat
moku

coral
puna

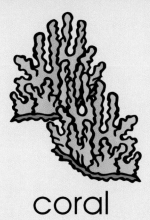

fish
i`a

dolphin
nai`a

turtle
honu

canoe
wa`a

whale
koholā

starfish
pe`a

seaweed
limu

jellyfish
pololia

shark
manō

surfer
he`e nalu

Let's Go Shopping

vegetables
lau`ai

basket
`eke

bag
`eke

fruit
hua

purse
pāiki

candy
kanakē

money
kālā

can
kini

carrots
kāloke

milk
waiū

wagon
ka`a

juice
wai

rice
laiki

banana
mai`a

pineapple
hala kahiki

chicken
moa

bread
palaoa

shave ice
haukōhi

poi
poi

eggs
hua

mango
manakō

mochi
mōchī

papaya
mīkana

Look at Me!

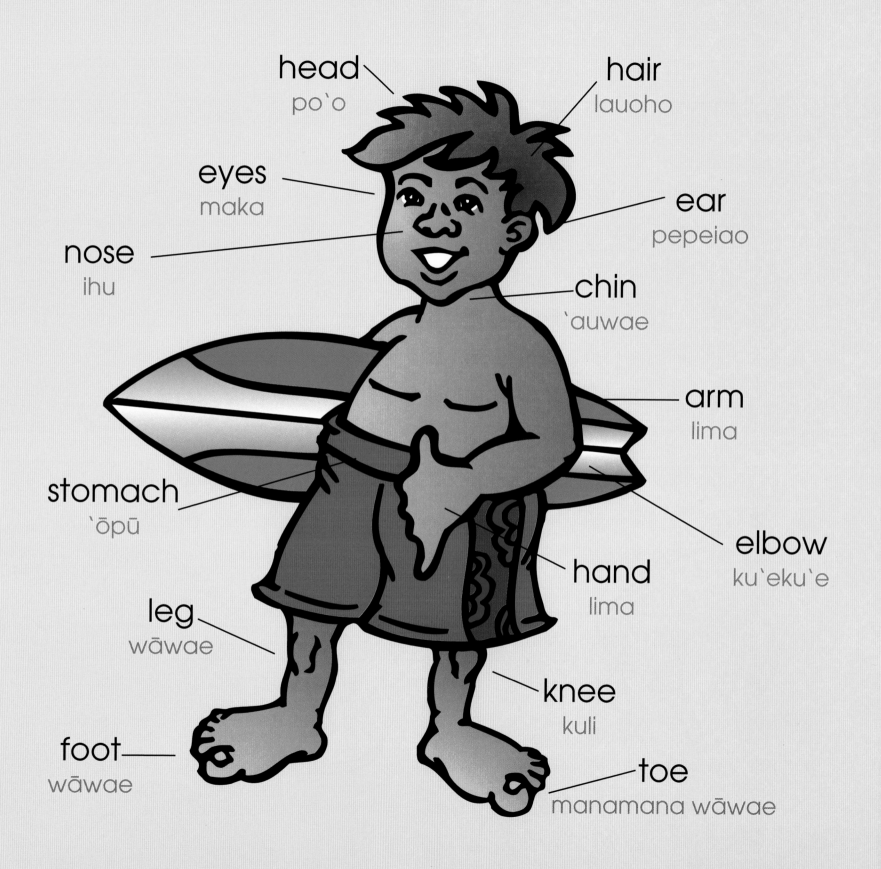

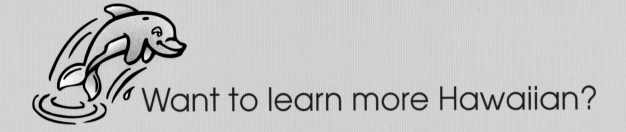

Want to learn more Hawaiian?

Reference these sources.

Pukui, Mary Kawena and Elbert, Samuel H. *Hawaiian Dictionary, Hawaiian-English English-Hawaiian, Revised and Enlarged Edition.* Honolulu: University of Hawaii Press, 1986.

Kōmike Hua`ōlelo, Hale Kuamo`o, `Aha Pūnana Leo. *Māmaka Kaiao, A Modern Hawaiian Vocabulary.* Honolulu: University of Hawaii Press, 2003.